CHEATING HEART

"Remember, the raffle is Friday night at the school dance," Claire told Ben.

Ben gave her hands a gentle squeeze. "I'll remember." Suddenly his face lit up. "You wouldn't consider going to the dance with me, would you? It sounds like fun. But it's your school, so you'll have to do the inviting."

Laughing, Claire said, "Would you like to go to the dance with me on Friday night, Mr. Hamilton?"

"Delighted, Ms. Diaz! I'll pick you up around seven-thirty." The next thing Claire knew, Ben's soft lips tenderly brushed her cheek. " 'Night, Claire," he said, his breath soft as a whisper against her skin.

As she walked inside, Claire wondered if she was dreaming. Had Ben really kissed her? And how was she ever going to wait until Friday night to see him again?

Bantam titles in the Sweet Dreams series. Ask your bookseller for any of the following titles you have missed:

15. THINKING OF YOU
16. HOW DO YOU SAY GOODBYE?
21. ALL'S FAIR IN LOVE
31. TOO CLOSE FOR COMFORT
32. DAYDREAMER
162. TRADING HEARTS
163. MY DREAM GUY
166. THREE'S A CROWD
167. WORKING AT LOVE
168. DREAM DATE
169. GOLDEN GIRL
170. ROCK 'N' ROLL SWEETHEART
174. LOVE ON STRIKE
177. THE TRUTH ABOUT LOVE
178. PROJECT BOYFRIEND
179. RACING HEARTS
180. OPPOSITES ATTRACT
181. TIME OUT FOR LOVE
182. DOWN WITH LOVE
183. THE REAL THING
184. TOO GOOD TO BE TRUE
185. FOCUS ON LOVE
186. THAT CERTAIN FEELING
187. FAIR WEATHER LOVE
188. PLAY ME A LOVE SONG
189. CHEATING HEART
190. ALMOST PERFECT
192. THE CINDERELLA GAME
193. LOVE ON THE UPBEAT
194. LUCKY IN LOVE
195. COMEDY OF ERRORS
196. CLASHING HEARTS
197. THE NEWS IS LOVE
198. PARTNERS IN LOVE
201. HIS AND HERS
202. LOVE ON WHEELS
203. LESSONS IN LOVE
204. PICTURE PERFECT ROMANCE
205. COWBOY KISSES
206. MOONLIGHT MELODY

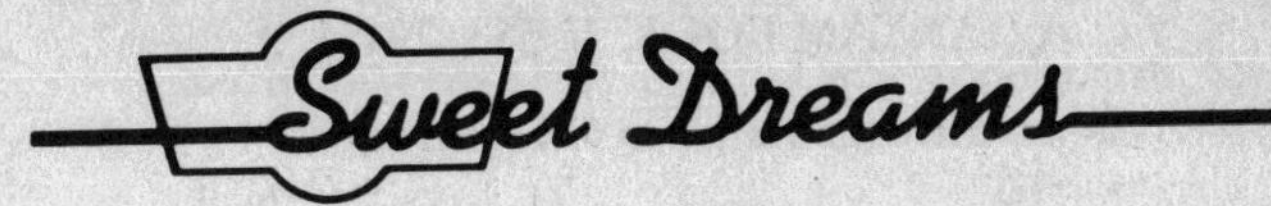

CHEATING HEART

Laurie Lykken

BANTAM BOOKS
NEW YORK • TORONTO • LONDON • SYDNEY • AUCKLAND

CHEATING HEART

A BANTAM BOOK 0 553 29451 2

First publication in Great Britain

PRINTING HISTORY
Bantam edition published 1993
Bantam edition reprinted 1995

Cover photo by Pat Hill

Bantam Books are published by Transworld Publishers Ltd, 61–63 Uxbridge Road, Ealing, London W5 5SA, in Australia by Transworld Publishers (Australia) Pty Ltd, 15–25 Helles Avenue, Moorebank, NSW 2170, and in New Zealand by Transworld Publishers (NZ) Ltd, 3 William Pickering Drive, Albany, Auckland.

Printed and bound in Great Britain by Cox & Wyman Ltd, Reading, Berkshire.

For Lindsay, Z'Leste,
and Madelyn. Keep reading!

Chapter One

"Oh, no," Claire Diaz muttered when she walked into her math room early Friday morning. It was only seven-thirty and Rob Meyers was already sitting at the computer terminal, hard at work. No matter how early Claire managed to get to Woodbury High, Rob got there first. In the past three weeks, she had only beaten him twice.

As soon as Claire spoke, Rob turned around and grinned. He obviously wasn't surprised to see her. She narrowed her brown eyes and glared at him.

"What are you doing here this early again?"

she demanded. "Why didn't you finish up yesterday?"

Rob grinned. "I did. Now I'm doing some extra-credit work. How about you? Are you behind or what?"

"Hardly," Claire snapped. She was getting madder by the minute. "I'm here to do extra-credit work, too."

Rob raised one dark eyebrow and cocked his head to the side, shaking it sympathetically. "It's too bad there's only one computer, isn't it?"

"It certainly is, particularly since you hog it all the time!"

Rob shook his head again. "Sorry. I wish I could turn the computer over to you now, but I can't. I probably won't be done with this much before school starts. Why don't you come back *after* school? I'm never here then."

"I'm not either. I work after school," Claire said.

"I work, too."

"I know," Claire said. "You work at Barker's Bagel Bakery." Woodbury was a very small town where most of the people knew everyone else's business.

Rob nodded. "Right. And that's why I come into school so early. Morning is the only time I have."

"I *have* to work," Claire pointed out self-righteously. She helped out in her family's jewelry store, Diaz Designs, after school and on weekends. "I don't have a choice. You, on the other hand, only work to support that car of yours."

Rob chuckled. "You think you know me pretty well, don't you?"

"I should. After all, I've known you a long time," Claire reminded him. *Too long*, she thought to herself but didn't say.

Rob nodded. "Ever since that accelerated math class back in grade school. Extra Work for Eggheads, as we used to call it."

Claire gave her long, black hair an angry toss. "*You* might have called it that. *I* never did. I liked that program."

Rob shrugged. "Did I say I didn't like it?"

Claire had had enough. She decided to come back to the math room at lunchtime.

If she was lucky, she'd be able to use the computer then. Meanwhile, she'd go to the library and find the books she needed for her American history paper on the suffragettes.

"Well, you better get back to work," she told him. "Hopefully, you'll do such a good job on that extra-credit work that you'll get yourself accelerated right out of here!" She turned and started out the door.

"Wait," Rob called after her, but Claire kept on moving. Rob Meyers might enjoy their verbal wars, but Claire Diaz didn't. It gave her a headache, and headaches made her eyes water, and when her eyes watered, she had to take out her contact lenses and put on her thick, ugly glasses.

Claire walked into the library and headed for the card catalog. She found the section she wanted and began to write down the titles of some reference books. Suddenly she had the feeling that she was being watched. Turning around, Claire saw Rob Meyers walking toward her.

"I'm through down there for now," Rob said loudly. Typically, he forgot to whisper.

"Shhh!" Claire hissed. "You're in a library!"

"Sorry," Rob said a little more softly. "I just thought you'd like to know that the computer is free now. It's all yours if you're still interested."

"Thanks," Claire said. "I appreciate it."

"What are you looking up?" Rob asked, moving closer to Claire.

"I'm doing a paper on the suffragettes," Claire answered. "For history. I have Ms. Thompkins."

"That's cool," Rob said. "I have Mr. Lester, and he'd never let us do a paper on chorus girls."

"The suffragettes are *not* chorus girls!" Claire shouted.

"Shhh!" She heard the librarian hiss.

Claire whispered fiercely, "The suffragettes were advocates of women's right to vote!"

Rob nodded. "Oh, yeah," he said. "I knew that. I guess I just forgot."

How, Claire asked herself, *could a boy who was so brilliant in math be so incredibly dense when it came to other things?*

"Well then," Rob said, "I guess I'll see you

in trig this afternoon." Trigonometry was the only class they shared, and as far as Claire was concerned, that was one class too many!

"Bye," Claire said, forcing herself to smile. "And thanks again for letting me know you were done with the computer."

She watched Rob saunter away. Maddening, aggravating, irritating, annoying—Rob Meyers was all those things and more!

"Headache?" Sandy Haberman asked on Friday afternoon when Claire sat down next to her on the bus.

"How did you guess?" Claire said. She opened her purse and took out the container for her contacts. She popped out each lens and dropped them into the container, then fished out her glasses and put them on.

The bus doors slid shut and the engine roared to life. Soon they were lurching down the street toward home.

"You have really nice eyes, Claire," Sandy said. "They're so incredibly dark. And you don't look as bad as you think you do in your glasses."

"Please," Claire said. "Can we talk about something else?"

"Okay," Sandy said cheerfully. "So have you reconsidered going to the basketball game with me tonight?"

Claire shook her head. "I don't like basketball."

"Do you think I do?" Sandy countered. "I'm not going to watch the stupid game. I'm going to see and be seen. We're *sophomores*, Claire. It's time for us to start having fun."

Claire just shrugged. She wanted her life to be more exciting, but spending a Friday night sitting on a hard wooden bench surrounded by screaming people didn't sound like fun.

"If you weren't my best friend," Sandy said as the bus pulled to a stop in front of Diaz Designs, "I'd give up on you."

"Have fun," Claire said as she stood up to get off. "And call me tomorrow. I want to hear all about it." She started down the aisle toward the door.

"If you'd come with us," Sandy shouted after her, "I wouldn't have to tell you anything!"

Claire walked around the corner and down the alley behind her family's store, then started up the wooden stairs leading to the apartment above.

As she unlocked the apartment door, she heard the family cat, Taxi, begin to yowl. Claire opened the door and went in. Ducking his orange head, Taxi rubbed himself adoringly against her legs.

"Is Paul home?" Claire asked the cat, but the quiet house answered for him. It was far too silent to contain a ten-year-old boy. Her parents, Claire knew, were in the store, where her mother worked behind the counter, and her father in the workroom, making the jewelry they sold.

Claire hurried into her room to change clothes before she went down to the store to relieve her mother. She peeled out of the black leggings and oversize turquoise top she'd worn to school and tossed them on her bed, then slipped on her favorite lime-green tights and put a denim miniskirt on over them. After she slipped on a pair of black flats, she said good-bye to her cat and headed down to the store.

Claire was just rounding the corner when a silver BMW pulled up in front of Diaz Designs. Three boys who looked to be slightly older than Claire got out. They were all wearing navy blue blazers with a silver-and-red crest on the pocket. They were obviously from Deacon Hill, the exclusive boys' boarding school on the outskirts of town.

"Something gold, I think," the boy who Claire had seen get out the driver's side of the car was saying as she entered the store.

"Why don't you look through the cases?" Mrs. Diaz suggested. "If something catches your eye, I'd be glad to take it out so you can have a better look."

He nodded in agreement and all three boys bent down, peering into the first display case.

"Hi, honey," Martha Diaz said to Claire. "How was your day?"

"Okay. Thanks again for driving me to school early," Claire said, watching the boys. The one who had been driving had rust-red hair and freckles. One of his friends was blond and the other one's hair was almost black. The dark-haired boy, Claire decided, was the best looking.

The boys moved on to the fourth case. Claire wondered if they really intended to buy something. She could tell that her mother was wondering the same thing. Spoiled—that's what Claire's dad called the boys from Deacon Hill, though Claire knew they all couldn't be that way.

Suddenly, the boy who had been driving looked up and said to Mrs. Diaz, "I'd like to see this pin, the one that's shaped like a magician."

"Ah. You mean Merlin," Mrs. Diaz said, smiling. Using a small key, she unlocked the case, took out the pin, and set it on a velvet cloth for the boy to examine.

"Get it, Fletch," the dark-haired boy advised. "Prissy will love it."

The boy called Fletch nodded thoughtfully. "Okay. I'll take it."

"Would you like to know how much it costs?" Mrs. Diaz asked.

Fletch pulled out a credit card. "I let my dad worry about that sort of thing," he said with an arrogant smile.

Mrs. Diaz rang up the sale, placed the pin into a small cotton-lined box, and then put it in a silver bag. She handed the bag to the redheaded boy.

"There you go," she said. "Enjoy."

"You made a good choice there, Fletch," the dark-haired boy said, giving his friend a slap on the shoulder. "Your sister's going to love it."

"Come again," Claire's mother called after the boys as they left, but they didn't acknowledge her.

Mrs. Diaz frowned. "Those boys have never had to work for anything in their lives. They're like hollow trees. Someday a big storm will come along, and over they'll go."

"Oh, I don't know," Claire said slowly. "We don't really know anything about them. Just because they live in a different world than ours doesn't mean they're bad." Then, thinking of the dark-haired boy, she added, "Maybe they're actually pretty nice once you get to know them."

Mrs. Diaz smiled. "You're right, of course, Claire. I guess I'm just a little jealous because they have so much more than my kids do. Well, now that you're here, I guess I'll run a few errands. I should be back in an hour or so. Dad's working on that opal set he promised to have done next week."

"Where's Paul?" Claire asked. Sometimes her brother was a big help around the store, but other times he was a pain in the neck. Claire never knew which he was going to be—it was a lot like living with a pint-size Dr. Jekyll and Mr. Hyde.

"He went to Elliot Berman's house after school so he won't be home until after we close," her mother said as she left.

When Claire was alone, she looked down at the spot where Merlin had been displayed and thought of Fletch and his credit card. *He probably has a computer of his own to work on at school. No waiting around for a few spare minutes of computer time! And no Rob Meyers to contend with.* Claire sighed. *Now that's luck!*

Chapter Two

"Claire!" Mrs. Diaz's voice rang down the hall on Sunday morning. "Sandy's here!"

Claire had been lying on her bed reading and Taxi was curled in a warm ball at her side. When she sat up, Taxi jumped off the bed and streaked out of the room.

"Send her back here," she shouted as the last of Taxi's orange tail shot out of sight.

"Hi," Sandy said a second later as she came into the room, "You missed a great game last night. What are you reading? Anything good?"

"It depends on what you mean by good."

Claire held up the book, one of those she'd found on the suffragettes.

"You are so far ahead of me on that history paper that I'm not sure I'll ever catch up," Sandy complained, throwing herself on the rug next to the bed. "Ugh," she exclaimed a moment later. "Cat hair! How do you stand it?" she asked, picking orange hairs off her purple leggings.

Claire shrugged. "You might say it grows on you."

Sandy smirked. "Very funny."

"Actually, Taxi is a great help. His purring keeps me focused on my reading. If I had a choice, though, I'd rather be working on the computer, which I can never do at school."

Sandy shook her head. "Ah, yes. Computer lack. I hear that's one of those *terminal* diseases."

Claire groaned at her friend's pun.

"Hey!" Sandy changed the subject. "Are you going to tell me why you summoned me over here? Or are you just going to let me guess?"

"Wait here," Claire commanded. She got

up and hurried into the living room. A moment later she came back with the family section of the Sunday paper.

"Here," Claire said, thrusting the newspaper at Sandy. "Look at that!"

"Canned peaches, two for a dollar," Sandy read. "So?"

"Not that. *This.*" Claire pointed at the box below the peaches ad. "Lind's is having a contest. The first group to collect fifty thousand dollars' worth of cash-register receipts and turn them in at the store will win a computer and a selection of educational software for their school."

"Okay," Sandy said. "What about it?"

Claire sat down on the rug next to Sandy. "Woodbury High really needs a second computer," Claire said. "And this is the way to get it. If we could win this contest quickly, we could have a new computer before spring break."

"I can see why *you're* interested," Sandy said. "But what's this got to do with me?"

"Winning a contest like this is going to take a lot of work," Claire told her. "It's going to take a lot of organization, and a lot of school spirit—more school spirit even than winning a basketball game."

Sandy nodded thoughtfully. "Collecting fifty thousand dollars' worth of cash-register receipts is definitely not going to be easy. That's a lot of groceries!"

"It just seems like a lot," Claire said. "If we can get everyone at Wooobury High to donate their family's receipts, I bet we could come up with the fifty thousand dollars pretty quickly. Right?" She grabbed hold of her friend's honey-colored braid and gave it a tug. "So, how about it? Are you in on this with me?"

"School spirit, huh?" Claire could tell that Sandy was weakening. "Oh, all right. Let's go for it! What have we got to lose?"

"Excellent!" Claire cheered. "We're going to do it! I just know we are! We'll get Valerie and Cheryl to help."

"Valerie, Cheryl, and who else?" Sandy demanded. "This is big, Claire. Very big. We need upperclassmen. We need *boys*."

"Good point," Claire said. "I knew I needed

you to pull this off, Sandy. Now I know why. You'll get the boys, right?"

"*We'll* get boys," Sandy corrected. "I mean, who sees more junior and senior boys every day than you? You take trigonometry with them. I mean, there's Rob Meyers for starters."

Claire shook her head. "No way, Sandy. Not Rob Meyers!" she said firmly.

"And why not? He's probably the one person who wants a second computer as much if not more than you do. He's a junior. He's good looking. He's . . ."

"A total jerk!" Claire folded her arms across her chest defiantly.

"Okay, then." Sandy stood up and started walking toward the door. "Be that way, Claire. But count me out. I don't want to put a lot of time into something that's hopeless from the start."

"This is blackmail," Claire said, getting up and going after her.

"Maybe it is," Sandy said over her shoulder. "But if you don't grab the opportunities that are right under your nose . . ."

"Okay, okay," Claire relented. "I'll talk to Rob tomorrow. Satisfied?"

"Yes," Sandy said, wearing a smile of victory. "Very!"

Claire spotted Rob right away Monday afternoon as she walked into her trigonometry class. She had been dreading this moment. Asking Rob to help out on the computer contest was going to be one of the hardest things she'd ever done—partly because Rob might turn her down, and partly because he might accept. Either way, she knew she wasn't going to be happy with the outcome.

Rob was talking to Jonathan Hillier, a senior, as Claire approached. He ignored her as she took the seat behind his. Finally Claire cleared her throat loudly, and he turned around.

Rob grinned and nodded at the computer at the front of the classroom. "No one's using it now," he joked. "Why not go for it?"

"I'm caught up at the moment," Claire said as pleasantly as she could. "But thanks for your concern."

"Speaking of concern," Rob said. "Where were you this morning? I was working here and you never even showed up."

"I was home," Claire said. "Unlike you, I don't have my own car."

"Hey," Jonathan said, cutting in, "anytime you need a ride, Claire, just holler."

"That's nice of you, Jonathan. Thanks."

"Don't mention it," Jonathan said.

"Have either of you guys heard about the contest Lind's is having?" she asked.

Jonathan nodded. "Yeah. I saw something about that in the paper yesterday. The first prize is a computer, isn't it?"

Rob looked interested. "Really? What does a person have to do to win this computer?"

"Eat fifty thousand dollars' worth of food," Jonathan said before Claire could get a word in.

Rob laughed. "I eat a lot, but not that much."

"It isn't what you think," she said. "The contest is aimed at groups, not individuals. The computer goes to a school, not one person." She opened her backpack and pulled out the ad she'd clipped from the paper. "Here," she said. "Read this."

"I see," Rob said, scanning the clipping.

"You both agree that Woodbury High could use a second computer, don't you?" Claire asked. "I mean, one computer for all of us to use is totally inadequate, right?"

Rob nodded. "Absolutely. But collecting fifty thousand dollars' worth of cash-register receipts is a tall order, even for a group."

"Of course it is. That's why we have to get the whole school involved." Claire watched Mr. Carlisle get up from his desk and pick up his chalk. "Look," she said quickly, "I'm holding an organizational meeting at my dad's jewelry store Tuesday afternoon right after school."

Rob nodded. "I know where that is."

"I don't," Jonathan said.

"It's on the corner of Forty-fourth and Upton," Claire told him.

"Count me in," Jonathan said.

"Great! How about you, Rob?"

"I can't make it," Rob said, sounding disappointed. "I've got to work."

"Okay, class," Mr. Carlisle said, rapping the chalk on the board. "Let's get started, shall we?"

"How about after work, then?" Claire whispered to Rob. "When do you get off?"

"Not until nine," Rob whispered back. "But I get a half-hour dinner break a little before eight. If you really can't get along without me, you could change your meeting to seven forty-five at the Bagel Bakery."

Claire scowled. *Why does he have to be so insufferably arrogant?* Just as she'd feared, involving Rob Meyers meant a major headache for her and probably all concerned. He always had to have things his way. He was a true egomaniac!

"I'll check with the others," Claire muttered.

"Did I hear you volunteer to put the first problem on the board, Ms. Diaz?" Mr. Carlisle asked, pointing at her. Claire felt her cheeks burn. Despite her embarrassment, she stood right up.

"I'd be glad to put the first problem on the board, Mr. Carlisle," she said, and walked up to the front of the room.

"Nice job, Claire," Mr. Carlisle commented when she'd finished and headed back to her seat. "I don't think this problem can be done in any fewer steps."

Rob Meyers's hand shot up.

"Yes, Mr. Meyers? Have you something to add?" Mr. Carlisle asked.

"I did that problem in fewer steps," Rob said. "*Two* fewer steps, to be exact."

"Really? I guess you better come up and show us. Put your solution right next to Claire's," Mr. Carlisle said.

Claire glared at the back of Rob's head the entire time he was writing. When he had finished, Mr. Carlisle said, "That's excellent, Mr. Meyers. Even I didn't see that possibility. Thank you."

With a big grin on his face, Rob sauntered back to his seat.

Claire wanted to scream. Rob had done it again! He'd shown her up. *Why?* she asked herself. *Does he just enjoy watching me squirm?*

"Mad?" Rob asked as everyone got up to leave at the end of class.

"Mad?" Claire repeated innocently. "Me? Why?"

"I don't know, but you look mad," Rob said.

"Hey, Claire," Jonathan interrupted. "I'll see you at your dad's shop tomorrow. Around four o'clock, right?"

"We might be meeting at the Bagel Bakery after dinner instead," Claire said grudgingly. "I'll let you know tomorrow, okay?"

"That's cool," Jonathan said as he walked off.

"Is that why you're mad?" Rob asked. "Because I have to work so you have to change your meeting?"

"I have to work, too," Claire snapped.

"In your parents' store," Rob pointed out. "When you work for your parents, you can't get fired."

"True, but you can't quit, either," Claire said.

Rob chuckled. "I guess I never thought of that."

"No," Claire said. "I guess you didn't. But it's true. You also don't get paid much."

"So, why do you do it?" Rob asked.

Claire's parents needed her help—the store was a family affair. But all that was too hard to explain, especially to someone like Rob who Claire thought only had an after-school job to pay for the luxury of a car.

"Hey!" he cried suddenly. "You're mad because you think I upstaged you with my alternate solution to that problem, aren't you?"

"Listen, I'd love to stick around denying all the reasons you can dream up for me being mad—which, by the way, I'm not. But I have a bus to catch," she said.

"Why don't you let me drive you home today?" Rob suggested. "That way I'll have plenty of time to apologize for whatever I did to make you mad. Maybe I can even convince you to forgive me. How about it, Claire?"

"No thanks," Claire said. She thought that if she had to spend one more moment with him, she'd die.

Rob shrugged. "Okay. Suit yourself. Maybe

you don't want me at the computer meeting tomorrow, either."

"That's where you're really wrong," Claire said, moving toward the door. "I *do* want you at that meeting, so I'm going to do everything I can to get the meeting moved to the Bagel Bakery."

"You made it," Sandy said as Claire collapsed on the bus seat a few minutes later.

"I was talking to Rob," Claire told her.

"I hope you were nice," Sandy said.

"I was nice," Claire assured her. "*Too* nice."

"So he's coming to our meeting then, right?"

"Only if we change the time and place for *him*," Claire said bitterly.

Sandy gave her a poke. "Lighten up, will you?"

"Sorry. Being nice to Rob isn't exactly the easiest thing in the world. It's given me a splitting headache."

"I don't understand it," Sandy mused. "Rob's cute. He's smart. He's . . ."

". . . a jerk!" Claire finished for her. "How many times do I have to tell you that before you start believing me?"

"I guess I'll just have to see for myself tomorrow," Sandy said. "Where and when?"

Claire sighed. "Barker's Bagel Bakery at a quarter to eight."

Chapter Three

"Where are you having this meeting?" Valerie Lane asked at lunch the next day, setting down her fork and reaching for her carton of milk.

"Barker's Bagel Bakery," Claire repeated and Cheryl James giggled.

"Did I say something funny?" Claire asked Cheryl, who shook her head but kept on giggling. Within moments, she had developed one of her infamous cases of hiccups.

"I'm not sure we should let her come to the meeting tonight," Sandy said.

"Who else is coming?" Valerie asked.

"Jonathan Hillier and Rob Meyers, us," Sandy said, indicating Claire and herself, "you . . . and any friends any of us can persuade to come."

"Jonathan is bringing a couple more seniors," Claire told them.

"Can I ask Mark Blessing?" Cheryl asked.

"Sure. Ask anyone you want," Sandy said quickly. "The more the merrier. Right, Claire?"

Claire nodded. The whole thing was out of her control now, but she didn't care. In fact, she was relieved. The major thing was winning that computer for Woodbury High, and the more people who got involved, the better—even if one of those people was Rob Meyers.

"They're here," Claire said, jumping up when she heard the honk.

"Aren't 'they' going to come up and get you? I think 'we'd' like to meet 'them,' " her father said.

"This isn't a date, Dad," Claire told him. "Jonathan is just a boy in my trig class who volunteered to drive people to our meeting tonight. He's a senior and he has his own car."

"You're going to Barker's Bagel Bakery on Forty-fourth and France, right?" Claire's mother asked.

"Yes, Mom," Claire said. She scooped up her purple parka and slipped it on.

"You'll be home before ten, of course," her father said. It was a statement and not a question.

"Of course," Claire said. "I know the rules." Being careful not to let Taxi escape into the night, she hurried out the door and ran down the stairs.

"At last," Jonathan said when Claire opened the back door of his metallic blue Chevy.

"Sorry I took so long," Claire said. She slid in next to a boy she'd seen around school but whose name she didn't know.

"Hi. I'm Bret Kelly," he said.

"I'm Claire Diaz."

Sandy turned around to face the backseat and waved. She was sitting between Jonathan and Deedee Chalmers, the captain of the cheerleading squad and undoubtedly the most popular girl in the senior class.

"Uh—aren't we headed in the wrong direction?" Claire asked as Jonathan turned a corner.

"We're picking up Valerie," Sandy explained. "That's why I'm sitting up here, so I can give Jonathan directions."

"Oh?" Deedee said coolly. "Is that why?"

When they got to Valerie's house, she ran out and climbed into the backseat.

"What about Cheryl?" Val asked. "Aren't we picking her up, too?"

"She's coming with Mark Blessing," Sandy explained. "Cheryl told me that Mark's really excited about the contest. She says he's got a million ideas."

A few minutes later, Jonathan pulled up to the Bagel Bakery. Claire was about to get out of the car when Deedee turned around. Smiling at Claire, she said, "Are you the math brain Jonathan's always talking about?"

Claire shrugged. "I don't know."

"You *are* in Jonathan's trig class, aren't you?" Deedee asked.

Claire nodded.

"But you're only a sophomore, right?" Deedee's voice seemed to imply that being a sophomore was even more peculiar than being a math brain.

"So?" Claire said. "What's your point, Deedee?"

"No point," Deedee said casually. She finally opened the car door and got out, followed by Sandy, Val, and Claire. Turning her attention to Jonathan and Bret, Deedee said, "Are you guys coming?"

"Go on in," Jonathan told her, as he noticed Rob's Chevy in the lot. "We'll be in, in a minute."

"Boys!" Deedee exclaimed as she led the way into the bakery.

Looking toward the counter, Claire saw Rob walking in their direction. "Hi, girls," he said. "I get off in ten minutes. We can start the meeting then." He pointed to Deedee, who was busily arranging the tables and chairs. "Is she going to be part of this contest thing, too?"

When Sandy nodded, Rob grinned enthusiastically. "All right!"

"Hey, Rob!" Jonathan called as he and Bret entered the bakery. "I noticed the new paint job on the Chevy. Looks great!"

"Thanks. It was a lot of work, but it's worth it," Rob said.

"The tables are ready back here," Deedee called out, motioning for everyone to join her.

Rob glanced up at the clock on the wall behind the counter. "My dinner break will start as soon as my boss gets back. Why don't you all go ahead and get started?"

"We're expecting a few other kids," Sandy explained. "We might as well wait."

"I'm getting something to drink," Jonathan said. "Anyone else want anything? Sodas all around—my treat."

While Jonathan waited at the counter for the sodas, a tall, thin boy with glasses walked in.

"Who's that?" Deedee asked, her nose wrinkling in distaste.

"Warren Kruggel," Valerie said. "He's in my German class. His family moved here last summer. He's some kind of super brain. Besides taking second-year German, he takes third-year Latin and first-year Spanish."

"I've seen him around school before," Claire said.

"Hey, Warren!" Rob called when he saw the boy. "You made it!"

Warren headed toward the counter to talk to Rob.

"Looks like he's here for the meeting," Deedee said, making a face.

A couple of customers came in, and Rob disappeared into the kitchen. Everyone else sat down at the tables Deedee had set up. Then Cheryl and Mark came in and joined them. When Rob's boss arrived, Rob came over and sat down with the committee.

"Okay," he said. "Let's get going. I've only got half an hour."

Sandy opened her purse and took out a stack of fliers. She kept one for herself and passed the rest along.

"Fifty thousand dollars' worth of receipts is

an awful lot," Deedee said, laying her flier down on the table next to her soft drink.

"But we can do it," Jonathan said confidently.

"Right," Rob agreed. "I think we should approach this just like any other money-making project."

"What do you mean?" Sandy asked him.

"Well," he said, turning to Deedee, "what do the cheerleaders do when they want to raise money?"

Deedee's face lit up. She was on familiar territory now. "Have a car wash."

Rob nodded. "Right. Have a car wash. Have a bake sale. Have a raffle."

"But we don't want to raise *money*," Bret pointed out. "We want to collect grocery-store receipts."

"But if we raised money, we could use it to buy groceries," Mark said, "for which we will collect receipts."

Deedee stared at Mark. "What are we going to do with all that food?"

"We'd donate it to the Food Bank. I volunteer over there twice a month and they're always low on stuff."

"I think that's a great idea," Claire said.

"I do, too. Besides being a good thing to do, tying in our effort to get a second computer with stocking the Food Bank will be great publicity for our cause," Rob said.

"We could also camp right outside of Lind's and ask people to give us their receipts," Valerie suggested eagerly. "We could make a big sign that says Support Your Local High School or something."

"Is someone writing this all down?" Warren asked, giving the black frames of his glasses a nervous poke. No one was.

"I'll be the secretary," Claire volunteered. She pulled her shoulder bag off the arm of her chair and took out a small notebook and a ballpoint pen.

"How about having a rummage sale?" Cheryl suggested. "They're really big this time of year."

"People can buy the stuff with Lind's receipts or money," Rob said. "Don't forget to write that down too, Claire."

Claire gave him a dirty look. She didn't need Rob Meyers telling her what to do. But he didn't seem to notice her annoyance.

By the time Rob's break was over, they'd managed to get an outline of a plan formulated. Claire promised to make copies of her notes for everyone.

"Do you think more of the cheerleaders might want to help out with this project, Deedee?" Rob asked as everyone stood up.

"Sure," Deedee said.

"I think we better not let the planning committee get any bigger than this," Sandy said. "But once we start in on these projects, we're going to need all the help we can get."

"Everyone here ought to head up one of the projects," Bret suggested.

"I've got to get back to work," Rob said, "but just tell me which project you want me to handle and I'll do it!"

Later, as Claire walked up the back stairs to the apartment, she found her thoughts drifting to Rob and the way he'd taken charge of the meeting. He had really impressed her. Claire wondered if she could be wrong about him. She'd seen tonight that there was a side to him that she'd never noticed before. Maybe the two of them would actually end up being friends. . . .

Chapter Four

"Don't worry about it, Mom. I can ride my bike to the car wash," Claire said on Saturday morning. She had just finished her breakfast and was eager to get on with the day's plans.

"Here, kitty," she called to Taxi as she took out a can of his favorite gourmet cat food. She set the cat's dish on the floor and walked back to the table to give her mother a hug.

"It's supposed to be a beautiful day," her mother said, returning the hug.

"Thank goodness for that blue sky," Claire said. "Our car wash would be a bust without it." She slipped on her parka, grabbed an apple from the bowl on the counter, and headed for the door.

"Bye, honey," her mother called after her. "Good luck."

When Claire got to the bottom of the stairs, she opened the back door of the shop, untangled her bike from Paul's and wheeled it out onto the sidewalk.

There was a chill in the early morning air and Claire soon began to wish she'd worn gloves. When she reached the school parking lot, the first thing she saw was Rob getting out of his Chevy. Claire coasted over and stopped next to him.

"Hi, you two!" Mark said, pulling up in his father's Toyota.

"Are you coming or going?" Rob asked him.

Cheryl's head popped out the window next to Mark's. "Both," she said. "We're on our way to put up more posters advertising the car wash."

"Need help?" Claire asked.

Mark shook his head. "No. We're picking up Val and the rest of the posters on the way. I think the three of us can handle things." He put the car in gear, and they roared off.

"So," Rob said. "Alone at last."

Claire laughed. "Not for long, I hope! Half the town of Woodbury better show up to have their cars washed." She wheeled her bike over to the nearest post and locked it up. "Where is everyone else?"

"They'll be along soon," Rob assured her. "Come on. I've got a ton of buckets, hoses, sponges, rags, and stuff in my trunk. You can help me carry it over to the turnaround."

"Please," Claire added.

"Huh?" Rob said.

"You forgot to say *please*," she said. "Everything you say sounds like an order."

Rob grinned sheepishly, the tips of his ears turning pink. "My mother and sister tell me the same thing."

"Maybe it's true, then."

"Okay. *Please*, Claire, help me carry all the junk in my trunk to the turnaround."

"Much better," Claire told him.

He began handing things to Claire until her arms were full.

"Where should I take this stuff?" Claire asked.

"Over there," Rob commanded. Then, apparently realizing he was giving orders again, he added, *"Please."*

Claire laughed. "This time you don't need to say please."

"Will I ever get it right?" Rob moaned jokingly. His arms were full now, too. They walked to the turnaround together.

"Eventually," Claire assured him. "Just like those suffragettes. They weren't good dancers at first. But after a lot of practice . . ." They dumped their loads on the grassy divider between the grade school and the bus turnaround.

Rob looked at Claire and scowled. "You're never going to let me forget that one, are you, Ms. Diaz?"

"I might," Claire said. "Provided you're willing to make a deal."

"Deal?" Rob asked, raising his eyebrows.

"I'm talking about the computer," Claire said.

"The new one or the old one?"

"The old one. We need to work out some sort of fair schedule," she told him. "Rushing in early day after day only to find you already there has been driving me crazy."

"You're right," he said. "In fact, I've even worked up a tentative schedule. I'll take Monday, Wednesday, and Friday mornings next week, and you can have Tuesday and Thursday. Then week after next we'll switch. This is just until we win the second computer, of course."

Claire nodded. "Of course."

"And," Rob said, waving at an old beat-up Chevy that was rumbling their way, "here comes our first customer!"

Claire laughed. "Wrong," she told him. "It's just Jonathan and Deedee."

A few minutes later, a big old Buick convertible rambled up behind Jonathan's Chevy and came to a screeching halt. Bret Kelly was driving, and with him were the other seven members of the cheering squad.

Mark and Bret hooked up the hoses and filled the buckets; Deedee handed out sponges to her troops; Rob gave Claire and her friends deerskin rags for drying the cars. The first car rolled up to be washed just as everything was organized. Jonathan hosed it down, and Deedee and the cheerleaders started soaping it up.

"I know I'm late," Warren said breathlessly as he rolled up just then on an ancient bike.

"That's okay," Rob said, handing him a scrub brush and a container of cleanser. "The important thing is that you're here."

From that moment on, cars came and went in a steady stream. By twelve o'clock, Claire's arms had begun to ache. She was also starving. "I think we need to eat something," she said. "Why don't I go for food and bring it back? I'll buy it at Lind's and save the receipt."

After collecting orders and money, Claire headed for her bike. She was just starting out of the parking lot when a car pulling in swerved so close to her that she was forced to tumble over to avoid being hit. As she lay on the pavement, dazed, she heard a voice that was vaguely familiar but which she couldn't quite place. "Are you all right?"

Claire slowly opened her eyes and found herself staring into a pair of wide-set, dark eyes, but the face above her looked fuzzy. Claire suddenly realized that she had lost both of her contacts when she'd fallen.

"My contacts!" she wailed.

"What happened? What's going on?" Rob's angry voice asked. He offered Claire a hand up.

"Are you all right, Claire?" Sandy asked anxiously.

"I'm fine," Claire said. "But my contacts . . ."

"Claire's lost her contacts," Sandy announced. "Look for them, everyone!"

All the kids got down on their hands and knees, searching for her contacts.

"Found one!" somebody called out a second later. Not long after that, someone else found the other one.

"Where are your glasses, Claire?" Sandy asked. "I hope they didn't get broken."

"I left them at home this morning," Claire

said. But she couldn't ride her bike to the apartment since she couldn't see without either her contacts or her glasses.

"I hope your contacts aren't scratched," the dark-eyed boy who'd been driving the car said. "If they are, I'll gladly pay to have them replaced."

"Get his name and phone number, Claire," Val whispered.

"Good idea," Sandy agreed. "I'll get a pen and some paper."

"Ben," the boy said when Sandy was ready to write. "Ben Hamilton."

"Ben," Claire repeated softly. Then suddenly she recognized him in spite of her blurred vision. He was the friend of the boy who'd bought the Merlin pin for his sister!

"I think you should go home, Claire, and rest," Sandy suggested.

"But what about everyone's lunch?" Claire asked.

"Don't worry about that," Rob told her.

"I'll drive you," Ben offered quickly.

"All right," Claire agreed against her better

judgment. "You'd better drive more carefully, though. The next person you nearly hit might not be so lucky!"

Rob laughed. "Sounds like Claire's back to her old feisty self," he said.

"Come on," Ben said, taking Claire by the elbow. "I'll put your bike in the trunk."

"I'll be back later," Claire promised her friends. She let Ben help her into his shiny silver car. She'd never been in such a fancy car before. She could tell the seats were covered in real leather.

"Where to?" Ben asked, sitting behind the wheel.

Claire told him her address, then added, "I live above Diaz Designs."

"*Now* I know why you look so familiar!" Ben exclaimed. "I saw you there the other day."

Claire nodded. "It's my parents' store. My dad's the one who designs."

She felt a little weird chatting like this with the boy who'd nearly run her down. But somehow, she found it impossible to stay mad at him. Anyway, it was an accident, pure and simple. Ben was being very nice about the whole thing, too.

"Well, here we are," Ben said a short while later as he parked in front of the store. He hopped out of the car and took Claire's bike out of the trunk.

"Thanks," Claire said, as she got out of the car.

"I'll put it away for you. Lead the way," Ben said.

They walked around the corner together and headed down the alley. When they reached the back door of the store, Claire opened it and Ben wheeled the bike in.

"You call me if there's anything wrong with your contacts," he said.

"Okay," she said, feeling suddenly awkward. It was time for Ben to go, but he wasn't acting like he was about to leave.

"So," he said, "what's the occasion for the car wash?"

"It's a fund-raiser," Claire said.

"Well, judging from the lineup of cars, I'd

say you were on your way to having a very successful operation."

"I hope so," Claire said.

"Where were you going? Were you finished working?" Ben asked.

"I was just running out for some sandwiches and stuff," she said. "I'm sure they'll manage without me until I can put my glasses on and get back over there."

"Want me to wait and drive you back?" he offered.

"Oh, no," Claire said. She suddenly felt very tired. She wanted to lie down with her eyes closed for a couple of minutes before going back. "Thanks anyway," she added. "I do appreciate everything you've done."

He turned around in the open door. "Everything except almost running you down to begin with, right?"

Claire laughed. "Right!"

"Well, I'll be seeing you," he said. His broad smile dazzled her despite her blurry vision. Then he left, closing the door behind him.

Chapter Five

"I had a great weekend!" Sandy said as the bus rumbled toward Woodbury High on Monday morning. Looking over at Claire dreamily, she added, "How about you?"

"Mmmm," Claire responded. Once again she saw the way Ben Hamilton had smiled at her just before he'd left the shop on Saturday. Meeting Ben had made everything that happened afterward seem special to her. Even playing checkers with Paul on Sunday night had seemed special!

"You and Rob certainly seemed to be hitting it off at the car wash," Sandy said.

Claire shrugged. "I think we've finally buried the hatchet. We've even worked out a way to share the computer until we get a second one. But that's as far as it goes."

Sandy abruptly changed the subject. "You know Matt Pearson, don't you?" she said.

"Of course. He's the editor of the school paper," Claire said. "Why?"

Sandy smiled and wiggled her eyebrows meaningfully. "You and *Matt Pearson*?" Claire shrieked.

Sandy nodded. "When I handed in my article on the Lind's contest Thursday, Matt asked if we needed extra hands at the car wash. I said sure, and he showed up! He came shortly after you left with that guy from Deacon Hill." She shook her head and frowned. "What a jerk that guy was! I still can't believe you got into his car with him."

Claire laughed. "You make it sound like he tried to run me over or something. It was just an accident, Sandy. He was really sorry. I can't tell you how many times he apologized."

"I guess you know more about it than I do.

Well, let's not waste time talking about *him.*" Sandy made a face. "Let's talk about the raffle next Friday night. I heard Rob got Lester's Car Emporium to donate a set of tires."

"I'm sorry I couldn't make it to the meeting yesterday," Claire said. "My parents had planned our shopping trip to Minneapolis weeks ago."

"That's okay," Sandy assured her. "Everyone understood." The bus stopped in front of the high school, and the girls stood up to get off. "The next meeting is tomorrow during lunch. Rob's getting the raffle tickets printed so we can start selling them tomorrow. Didn't he call you? He said he was going to."

"No," Claire said. "He didn't."

"You know, Claire," Sandy said as she followed Claire into the building, "you could do a lot worse than Rob Meyers. I really think you should rethink your position on him."

Claire spun around. "Look, Sandy," she said angrily. "Quit trying to push Rob Meyers on me, okay?"

"Okay, okay," Sandy said. "Don't bite my head off!"

She started up the stairs to the second floor, but Claire hung back.

"You go on," Claire said. "I just remembered something I have to do before school starts."

Before Sandy could ask any questions, Claire hurried away. She didn't really have anything special to do. She'd just wanted to get away from Sandy. She was glad that Sandy liked Matt Pearson and that Matt liked Sandy, too. But she didn't have to like Rob now just because Sandy was interested in someone.

Claire glanced up at the hall clock. She had nearly fifteen minutes before her first class, so she decided to go to the math room on the outside chance that she could spend a few minutes on the computer.

When Claire reached Mr. Carlisle's room, however, she found Rob still at work. She wasn't surprised. After all, they had agreed on Saturday that Monday, Wednesday, and Friday would be Rob's days this week.

"Hey," Rob said, suddenly spinning around

and seeing Claire standing in the doorway. "Hi, Claire. What's up?"

Sandy was right, Claire thought grudgingly. Rob was pretty cute. *Very* cute, in fact.

"What can I do for you?" he asked. "This *is* my morning, isn't it?"

"Yes," Claire agreed. "I just thought you might be done."

Rob shook his head. "Sorry."

"Okay." Claire turned away, about to go out the door.

"Wait," Rob said. He pushed back his chair and stood up. "I thought I'd offer you a ride tomorrow morning since I'll be coming in early myself, anyway."

"That's very nice of you," Claire said, surprised.

Rob blushed a little and shifted uneasily from one foot to the other. "Niceness isn't really what motivated my offer," he confessed.

"No? Then what *is* your motivation?"

"Well, to be honest, I'm right in the middle of something here that I hate to leave until Wednesday. I was hoping you might let me have a little of your time if I helped you get here early."

Claire grinned. Cute or not, Rob was the same jerk he'd always been—totally out for himself.

"Okay then," she agreed. "I'd be glad to ride with you." She started to leave again.

"Wait," Rob said. "There's more."

"What?" Claire asked, annoyed.

"It's about the raffle. We'd like your father to donate some jewelry—you know, like earrings or something."

"I'll ask him about it," Claire promised, glancing at the clock. She had only a few minutes to get to her first class.

"Can you let me know tonight? I'll call you, okay? I'm printing the tickets, and I'd like your dad's donation to be noted on them."

Claire nodded, left the room, and started down the hall.

"Claire!" Paul bellowed, even though he was less than ten feet away from her. "Telephone!"

Claire set down the pen she'd been using to copy over her lab notes and frowned at her parents. "I wish you'd teach that kid some manners," she grumbled. She stood up, nearly falling over Taxi.

"Claire!" Paul yelled again. Claire hurried into the kitchen to get the phone.

"It's a boy," Paul said loudly, making his eyes big and round as he held out the receiver. Claire snatched it from him.

"Hello?" she said, turning her back on Paul.

"Claire? It's me. Rob."

"Oh," Claire said. She'd guessed it would be Rob—he had told her he'd call. But still, a little piece of her had hoped the call was from Ben.

"I'm calling to see if your dad's decided on his donation to the raffle," Rob said.

"He said no problem. How's a pendant and earrings?"

"Great! So what time should I pick you up tomorrow?"

"Is seven too early?" she asked.

"How about seven-thirty?" Rob answered.

"All right. But I can't promise you any of my computer time then."

"You drive a hard bargain, Diaz." Rob sighed, then said, "All right—seven o'clock it is. But you better be ready when I get there."

"If I'm not, you can leave without me and steal *all* my computer time," Claire told him.

"It's a deal. I'll see you tomorrow then," Rob said.

"Who was that, Claire?" her father asked.

"Just a guy calling about the contest," Claire said. "You know, the computer contest Lind's is having." Her family continued to look at her expectantly. "Well, for Pete's sake," Claire cried out in frustration. First her best friend and now her family! Was everyone trying to pair her up with Rob?

She turned away from them and stormed into her room, slammed the door, and threw herself across her bed.

Claire was just beginning to regret her outburst when there was a soft rap on the door. "Claire?" her mother said. "It's the phone again, honey. Shall I tell whoever it is to call back?"

"Who is it?" she asked.

"I don't know who it is, honey. But it's

definitely male." Mrs. Diaz responded. "Maybe it's the boy who called before."

"Can I take it in your room, Mom?" Claire asked.

"Of course," Mrs. Diaz agreed. "I'll hang up the kitchen phone when I hear you on the line."

Claire opened the door. "Thanks, Mom," she said sheepishly. "I'm sorry I yelled at everyone like that before."

"Apology accepted," her mother said, smiling.

As soon as Claire picked up the receiver in her parents' room, she heard her mother hang up.

"Hi, Claire. This is Ben Hamilton." His voice sounded smooth and confident. "We met at the car wash the other day, remember?"

Claire gave a little gasp. "Oh, I remember," she managed to say.

"How are you?" Ben asked. "Have you recovered from our accident?"

"One hundred percent," Claire assured him. "And my contacts weren't even scratched."

"I'm glad. I've been thinking about you ever since I left your place on Saturday. I went back to the car wash and heard that your school is trying to win that computer in the Lind's contest."

"That's right," Claire said.

"If you don't mind me asking, how close is Woodbury High to winning it?"

"Not too close yet," Claire told him. "But we're having a big raffle Friday. I hope we'll be closer after that. We're using the money we make to buy groceries at Lind's for the Food Bank. Raffle tickets go on sale tomorrow," she added. "Interested in buying any? There's going to be a set of tires from Lester's in the raffle among other things."

"A lot of guys at school might be interested. How much are those tickets going to cost?"

"Only a dollar apiece," Claire said. Then she went on to list some of the other prizes in the raffle.

"I bet I could sell fifty tickets here at Deacon Hill," Ben said. "Probably more. I'll buy ten of them myself."

"That would be super!" Claire exclaimed.

"Look, get me fifty to start with, okay?"

"Fifty it is," Claire said. "Will you pick them up tomorrow?"

"Sure. We could go for ice cream or something at the same time—I mean, if you'd like to."

Claire drew in her breath. Ben Hamilton was actually asking her out! "That sounds nice," she said as casually as she could manage.

"How about eight o'clock tomorrow night, then?"

"Eight o'clock sounds perfect," Claire said.

"I have to be in by ten-thirty," Ben warned. "It's the rule at Deacon Hill."

Claire laughed. "I have to be in by ten, so it'll be fine."

"See you tomorrow, then," Ben said.

They said goodbye, and Claire hung up.

Claire reached for the phone again and started to dial Sandy's number. But before she'd even punched in the first three digits, she hung up. She wasn't ready to tell anyone about Ben yet. No one, not even Sandy, would understand how Claire could be excited about going out with a boy who'd nearly run her over!

When Claire went into the living room, her parents were reading, and her brother was doing his homework. She couldn't wait to tell them she had a date for the following night. But they didn't look up.

"Well, for Pete's sake!" she said, planting her hands indignantly on her hips. "Isn't anyone going to ask me who that was?"

Mrs. Diaz laughed. "We all wanted to know," she said, "but we were afraid to ask. Who was it?"

"His name is Ben Hamilton and he goes to Deacon Hill," Claire blurted out excitedly. "You've seen him before, Mom. He was in the store the other day with that boy who bought Dad's Merlin pin."

"Deacon Hill?" Mr. Diaz said, scowling. "You met this boy in the store?"

"Well, no," Claire said. "Not exactly. I met him at the car wash on Saturday. But we remembered each other from the store. He asked me out!"

"He did, did he? When?" her father asked, still scowling.

"Tomorrow night," Claire replied.

Mrs. Diaz shook her head. "I don't know, Claire. It's a school night. You need to be home by ten."

"I know. I will be," Claire promised.

"Deacon Hill," Mr. Diaz said again, shaking his head as if he couldn't quite believe it.

"There's nothing wrong with Deacon Hill," Claire said defensively. Her parents had to be crazy. Why weren't they happy for her? Any girl who had a chance to date a good-looking boy from Deacon Hill was lucky. Surely they knew that as well as she did.

Chapter Six

Claire was in the bathroom brushing her teeth Tuesday morning when she heard the doorbell ring. Rob! She'd been so busy planning for her date that evening with Ben, she'd forgotten all about riding to school that morning with Rob!

She was quickly running a comb through her hair when there was a knock on the bathroom door.

"Your friend is here, Claire," her father called in to her.

"Thanks, Dad. I'm coming," Claire called

back. She tossed the comb on the edge of the sink and headed out to meet Rob.

She heard Rob introducing himself as she reached the living room. Her family had him surrounded and were giving him the third degree. Even Taxi was looking him over. Claire rushed to the rescue.

"I thought your name was Ben," Paul said before she could intervene.

"Nope," Rob said, letting Paul's comment roll right off his back. "It's always been Rob. Always will be, too."

"Hi, Rob," Claire said. "I see you've met my family."

"Yes," Rob said. "Ready to go?"

"But you haven't eaten breakfast yet, Claire," Mrs. Diaz protested.

"There's no time now, Mom," Claire said, practically pushing Rob through the door in her eagerness to escape. "Rob and I have to get to school so we have plenty of time to use the computer."

"Oh, so you go to Woodbury High, too." Mr. Diaz sounded relieved.

"Wait." Her mother stopped her. "At least

take an apple with you. You have to eat *something.* How about you, Ben? Can I get you an apple, too?"

"His name isn't Ben, Mom. It's *Rob,*" Paul whispered loudly.

"Of course," Mrs. Diaz said, looking embarrassed. "You just told us that, didn't you, Rob? Well, would you like an apple, too?"

Rob nodded. "Sure." Being called Ben over and over again didn't seem to bother him. "That would be very nice. Thank you."

When they finally got down to his car, each of them was holding an apple.

"I'm sorry my folks put you on the spot like that. I mean, they act like they never see people or something. Really, they see people all day long in the store!" Claire said, laughing nervously.

Rob gave a shrug. "I caught them off guard. Everyone acts a little weird when they're caught off guard. Things can get pretty strange around my place, too. My mom has started dating, and I can't remember the guys' names, either. They all sound alike—Bruce, Bob, Bill, Brad."

"Are your parents divorced?" Claire asked without thinking.

Rob shook his head. "No. My dad died a couple years ago. It was very sudden. One day he was fine and then the next day he died of a heart attack."

"I didn't know," Claire said softly. "I'm sorry."

"It was rough for a while," Rob admitted. "But things have settled down now. Luckily my sister, Joan, got a scholarship that pays most of her college expenses. And I have my job at the Bagel Bakery. I keep some of what I make, but I give most of it to Mom."

"Oh, Rob!" Claire exclaimed. "You aren't just working to have a car like I thought you were."

Rob smiled. "Hey, I don't mind working. It's helped me prioritize my life, know what I mean?"

Claire nodded. "I guess helping out at our store does that for me, too."

When Rob pulled his Chevy into the school parking lot, Claire started to get out, but Rob put his hand on her shoulder.

"Wait, Claire. I don't want you to get the wrong idea and start feeling sorry for me," he said.

Turning, Claire replied honestly, "I don't feel sorry for you, Rob. In fact, I admire you."

Rob let go of Claire's shoulder and threw himself back against the seat. "Gimme a break!" he cried. "*Admire* me? That's even worse!"

Claire laughed. "I'm sorry. I'll try *not* to admire you, then, okay?"

"Please," he said. "You've got to do more than try. You've got to promise."

Claire said, "All right. I promise I'll try." They were both laughing as they got out of the car.

"So, how much computer work do you have exactly?" Rob asked as they headed into the school.

"A lot, I'm afraid," she said.

Rob shrugged. "That's okay. I'm going to the library. Would you come up and get me when you're done?"

"Sure. Oh, wait. I need five raffle ticket

books before the end of the day," Claire called after him.

"They should be ready by lunchtime. I'm hoping to dole them out then. I'll set aside five books for you," Rob promised.

"Thanks. See you." Claire waved and turned to leave. She had a feeling that Rob was watching her walk away, but she didn't want to turn around to make sure.

"Rob is coming this way!" Sandy hissed, giving Claire a little kick under the lunch table.

"Ow!" Claire cried, tossing down the carrot stick she'd been nibbling. "Knock it off, or I'm going to move to another table, I swear!"

"Ladies," Rob said, setting down a shoe box on the table. "Here they are! Raffle tickets! Don't all grab at once. There are more than enough to go around." He pulled out a book and waved it at them. "There are ten tickets to a book. Just tell me now how many books you want to sell. Two? Three? Ten?"

"One," Valerie said, holding out her hand.

"One!" Rob complained as he deposited the book of tickets he was holding in her hand. "Only one? Look at the prizes, Valerie. They are truly fabulous!"

"Well, I'll take one," Cheryl said. Rob looked disappointed. "Sorry," she said. "I want to see how well I do before I commit to accepting more."

"I'll take one, too," Sandy added.

"Well, at least Claire has some ambition," Rob said, as he carefully counted out five books.

"Better make that six," she said.

"Six!" Sandy exclaimed.

"Five of them are already sold," Claire explained.

"I'm impressed!" Rob said, as he put the lid back on his shoe box. "Well, I better move on. See you in trig, Claire. Bye, girls." He walked to another table where he immediately launched into his pitch again.

"Okay," Sandy said to Claire as soon as Rob was gone. "What gives?"

"Nothing," Claire said innocently. "Nothing at all."

"You haven't really sold five books already, have you?" Cheryl asked.

"Yes, I have," Claire said. "And I'm sure I can sell a sixth while I'm working in the store."

"Who did you sell them to?" Sandy demanded.

Claire shook her head. "I can't tell you just yet." She stood up and picked up her tray.

Sandy started to stand up, too. "I'll go with you," she said.

But Claire shook her head. "Don't bother," she said. Then realizing how harsh she'd sounded, she added, "I'm on my way to use the computer. See you later," she added for the benefit of her other two friends.

Claire got her books from the shelves outside the cafeteria. As she walked down to the math room, she mused that in just a few hours she was going to see Ben again. And that thought made a funny little tingle run down her spine.

"How do I look, Mom?" Claire asked that evening. It was nearly eight o'clock. Ben would be arriving any minute now.

Mrs. Diaz raised her eyes from her accounting books and said, "You look just fine, Claire. Everything you had on before looked fine, too."

"So, do you think I look too casual?" Claire asked anxiously. Her mother shook her head. "Too dressy?" Again, Mrs. Diaz shook her head. Claire looked down at her clothes. "How about cat hair? Do you see any?"

"You look lovely," her mother assured her. "Besides, I don't think the boy will notice a little cat hair."

The doorbell rang just then and Claire squealed, "He's here!" For a moment, she actually thought she might faint.

"Relax, honey," her mother advised. "Do you want me to let him in?"

"No." Claire took a deep breath, then slowly exhaled. "I'll do it." She was glad that her father and brother were at Paul's Cub Scout meeting so they couldn't embarrass her to death.

She opened the door, and Ben stepped into the apartment. He looked slowly around the living room. Then, smiling at Claire, he said,

"It's neat that you live right above your store. It's like something out of a movie."

"Hello, Ben," Mrs. Diaz said, walking toward him, her hand outstretched. "I'm Claire's mother."

Ben took her hand and gave it a brief, firm shake. "It's nice to meet you, Mrs. Diaz."

"Would you two like something to drink? I was just about to make myself a cup of tea."

"Thank you, Mrs. Diaz," Ben said politely. "It's nice of you to offer. But I promised Claire I'd take her out for ice cream. I have to be back at school by ten-thirty, so we should probably get going."

"Claire has a curfew, too. Ten o'clock," her mother said pointedly.

"Don't worry, I'll have her back by ten," Ben promised. He took Claire's hand, taking her breath away in the process. She felt giddy. Nothing in her life before this moment had been nearly as exciting.

"I thought we'd go to Clancy's," Ben said a couple of minutes later, as he started his car. "Is that all right with you?"

"That would be fine," Claire agreed.

"What's your favorite flavor of ice cream?" he asked. "My all-time favorite is this ice cream I had once in New York. It had cherries and almonds in it and ribbons of fudge running all through it. It was like eating a little piece of heaven."

"New York City?" Claire asked. "I bet you've been to all sorts of interesting places."

"I've traveled some. But really, every place is pretty much the same after a while," Ben said. "But I'd much rather talk about you."

Claire felt flattered. "All right. What would you like to know?"

"Well, how about telling me some more about this raffle? Was it your idea?" They'd reached Clancy's, an old-fashioned drugstore with a large soda fountain in the back, and Ben pulled into the parking lot.

"No," Claire admitted. It had been Rob's idea, but Claire didn't want to talk about Rob with Ben.

Before she could open her own door, Ben opened it for her. He offered her his hand

and helped her out. Then, with her hand still in his, they walked into Clancy's.

The place was unusually busy for a Tuesday night. The crowd, Claire noted as she looked around, was mostly Woodbury seniors.

"I see an empty booth," Ben said. "We better hurry before someone else takes it."

"So," Ben said as soon as they were in the booth sitting across from each other, "did you get those raffle tickets for me?"

"Thanks for reminding me," Claire said. She opened her shoulder bag and took out the five books of tickets. "Are you sure you still want all of these?"

Ben nodded. "Absolutely. I've already sold them. The guys at school were pretty excited about the whole thing. It can get pretty dull at The Hill, you know." He pulled out his wallet and took out a fifty-dollar bill. "Here you go," he said, handing the bill to Claire. He picked up a book of tickets and looked it over for a second, smiling. "Good," he said. "The prizes are listed right on the tickets just as I'd hoped they'd be."

"Rob thought listing the prizes would be a good sales tool," Claire told him.

"Rob?" Ben said. "Who's he?"

"Just a guy on the committee," Claire said.

"Yo! Claire!" Claire looked up to see Jonathan coming over to their table.

"Hi, Jonathan," she said.

Jonathan held out his hand to Ben and said, "Jonathan Hillier. I don't believe we've met."

"Ben Hamilton," Ben said, shaking Jonathan's hand.

"Are you a sophomore?" Jonathan asked.

Ben shook his head. "Actually, I'm somewhere between a junior and a senior."

"Really?" Jonathan sounded skeptical.

"Really," Ben assured him. "I go to Deacon Hill."

"Ben just sold fifty of our raffle tickets," Claire told Jonathan. "Isn't that terrific?"

Jonathan frowned. "Yeah—terrific."

"Hey, Jon!" one of the boys at the video machines called out. "It's your turn over here, man."

"Looks like I have to go," Jonathan said. "Nice to meet you, Ben. Catch you later, Claire."

After he had left, Ben said, "Why do I get the feeling your friend didn't like me?"

"It isn't anything personal," Claire assured him. "It's just that a lot of guys at Woodbury High are kind of suspicious of the boys from Deacon Hill." She hoped Ben wouldn't be offended, and apparently he wasn't. He just laughed, and motioned to a passing waitress.

They both decided on hot fudge sundaes. After the waitress had brought their order, Claire asked Ben to tell her what Deacon Hill was like, and he was more than happy to give her plenty of details. She found his stories fascinating, almost forgetting to eat her ice cream as she listened. And when Ben asked her a lot of questions about Woodbury High's strategy to win the computer, he listened to her answers just as closely.

"It's getting late," Ben told her at last, glancing at his watch. "We'd better get going. I don't want you to miss your curfew."

Looking down at her own watch, Claire saw it was indeed close to ten o'clock. Time had passed so quickly!

"I'm ready," she said. "The sundae was delicious. Thanks."

"You're welcome. And thank *you* for getting me these tickets." Ben patted the pocket holding the raffle tickets.

Claire smiled. "I really ought to be thanking *you* for that, don't you think?"

"Maybe, maybe not. Someone from Deacon Hill might just walk away with all the prizes!"

"I hope at least one of those fifty tickets is a winner," Claire said.

Ben grinned at her. "Don't worry about that, okay? I feel lucky."

When they got back to Claire's, it was exactly ten o'clock. Ben walked her up the stairs to the apartment.

"I had a nice time tonight, Claire," he said, taking her hands in his. A warm current traveled all through her, and Claire smiled dreamily.

"I did, too," she said softly.

"We'll have to do this again. I really appreciate your letting me in on the raffle."

"Remember, it's Friday night at the school dance," Claire told him. "You'll have to get the filled-out stubs back to me before then or they won't be part of the drawing."

Ben gave her hands a gentle squeeze. "I'll remember." Suddenly his face lit up. "You wouldn't consider going to the dance with me, would you? It sounds like fun. But it's your school, so you'll have to do the inviting."

Laughing, Claire said, "Would you like to go to the dance with me Friday night, Mr. Hamilton?"

"Delighted, Ms. Diaz! I'll pick you up. What time?" he asked.

"How about seven-thirty?" she suggested. "The dance doesn't start until eight, but we'll need to find a place to park."

"Claire," Ben said softly, "you're wonderful. It was my lucky day when I ran into you!" The next thing Claire knew, Ben's soft lips tenderly brushed her cheek.

" 'Night, Claire," he said, his breath soft as a whisper against her skin. Then, before

Claire could think of anything to say, he was running down the stairs to the street.

As she walked inside, Claire wondered if she was dreaming. Had Ben really kissed her? And how was she ever going to wait until Friday night to see him again?

Chapter Seven

"How was your date last night, Claire?"

Claire spun around to face Sandy Haberman. She bumped her locker door shut with her knee and sighed. "Who told you?" she asked.

"Does it matter?" Sandy scowled. "I mean, it obviously wasn't you. That's what gets me! I thought we were best friends."

"I was going to tell you—" Claire began.

"When?" Sandy demanded. "Next year?"

"Today. Anyway, I knew you'd take it like this." Claire was starting to feel angry, too. "That's why I didn't tell you before."

"So tell me now. Who is he? Do I know him?"

"Didn't Jonathan tell you that, too?" Claire asked. "I introduced them."

"Jonathan Hillier met him?" Sandy asked, surprised.

"You mean you didn't find out from Jonathan?"

"No. Maggie Harper told me she saw you with some guy at Clancy's last night," Sandy said. "According to Maggie, you looked like you'd died and gone to heaven."

Claire couldn't help smiling. "I had a wonderful time," she admitted.

"Who were you with?" Sandy asked. "You *are* going to tell me, aren't you?"

Claire sighed dreamily. "Remember the guy who nearly ran me over at the car wash?"

Sandy gasped. "*Him?* You went out with *him*?"

Claire nodded. "And he's taking me to the dance on Friday, too. Ben's really nice, Sandy. You'll love him."

"Claire!" she heard Rob call, and looked up to see him heading in her direction.

Claire opened her purse and took out Ben's fifty-dollar bill.

"What's that?" Sandy asked, her eyes widening.

"It's the money for the raffle tickets Ben paid me for last night," Claire explained. As Rob joined them, she handed him the fifty-dollar bill. "I sold those five books of raffle tickets."

Rob looked impressed. "All right! Where are the stubs?"

"I'll have them for you in time for the drawing Friday night," Claire promised.

"Now that you brought it up, I'd like to talk to you about Friday night," Rob said. He cleared his throat and looked nervously at Sandy.

"Will it take long?" Claire asked. "I need to ask Mrs. Havirilla a few questions about my biology notes. If I don't go right now, I might miss her."

"Okay," Rob said. "Maybe I'll see you at lunch." He started off down the hall.

As soon as he was safely out of earshot, Sandy cried, "Shame on you, Claire Diaz! You're leading him on!"

"What are you talking about?" Claire asked, genuinely bewildered.

"You should have told him you already have a date for Friday night," Sandy said. "He obviously wants to ask you to the dance."

"You're imagining things, Sandy," Claire said. "You really are. Rob's not interested in me."

"Yes, he is," Sandy countered. "Rob likes you, Claire. He likes you a lot."

"Okay, I'll tell Rob I have a date, but I promise you he isn't going to care. At least, not the way you think."

Claire was walking past Mr. Carlisle's room on her way to meet Sandy for lunch a couple of hours later, when she spotted Rob hurrying toward her.

"Can I talk to you about Friday night?" he asked when he reached her. "The raffle is Friday night, and I—"

"I know," Claire interrupted. Then, before she could chicken out, she quickly added, "I have a date for the dance."

Rob said cheerfully, "Well, that's great! But

I was hoping you wouldn't mind helping me with the drawing. You *don't* mind, do you? I mean, it wouldn't interfere with your date, would it?"

"No. I'd be glad to help," Claire said, feeling oddly disappointed.

"Have you bought raffle tickets for yourself yet?" Rob asked.

"No," Claire replied. "Not yet."

"Good!" Rob said. "Don't. If you don't buy any tickets, you can do the actual drawing of the winners. I *did* buy a couple of tickets, so I don't think I should do the drawing. It might look funny if I pulled out my own winning ticket."

"That makes sense," Claire said. "Are you going to lunch?"

Rob shook his head. "I'm going to work on the computer."

"Well, I guess I'll see you in trig then," she said as they went their separate ways.

As she walked to the cafeteria, Claire felt happier than she'd ever felt before in her life. She had her date with Ben to look forward to, and that was wonderful. But knowing that her date with Ben didn't mean ending her budding friendship with Rob was equally wonderful. She felt suddenly that she had it all.

When the doorbell rang Friday night, Paul shouted, "I'll get it!" Flying out of the kitchen, he raced toward the door. "Don't worry, Claire," Paul said, reaching for the doorknob. "I won't call the guy Ben."

"But it *is* Ben this time," Claire cried. Before Claire could stop him, Paul opened the door.

"Hi," he said sweetly. "You must be Ben."

"And you must be? . . ."

"I'm Paul, Claire's brother," Paul said, puffing out his thin chest importantly.

"So," Ben said, "where's Claire? Oh, hi there," he said as soon as he spotted her.

"Hi, Ben," Claire responded. She thought he looked terrific in dark brown cords and a white button-down shirt, topped with a brown leather bomber jacket. She was awfully glad that she had decided to wear her brown-and-gold paisley skirt and the gold-colored top. Their outfits went perfectly together.

"Maybe we should go," Claire said after a few minutes. "Parking close to the school might be a problem tonight."

"Any particular time Claire should be home?" Ben asked, looking from Claire's mother to her father.

"Midnight," her parents said at exactly the same time. Everyone, including Paul, laughed. Ben and Claire said their good-byes and left.

"I like your family," Ben said as he helped Claire into his car. "You're lucky. I don't have any brothers or sisters, and my parents haven't spoken to each other in years. They hardly even speak to *me* much anymore. But, aside from that, I'd have to say I have everything I want. I guess that makes me lucky, too."

Not knowing what to say, Claire simply said, "Oh." They rode the next couple of blocks in silence. When they reached the school, Ben parked a block away.

"Would you mind visiting with some of my friends?" she asked as they walked toward the school gym.

"Of course not," Ben said. "I've never gone to a regular high school thing like this. I want to do it right."

Claire laughed. "You make it sound like you're on some kind of exotic safari or something!"

Ben shrugged. "I guess in a way that's what it is for me. Do you mind?"

"No," Claire said. "I don't mind. I just want you to enjoy yourself."

When they entered the gym, Claire waved at Sandy and Matt who were standing by a refreshment table in the corner. She led Ben over to them.

"This is my best friend, Sandy Haberman," she told Ben. "And this is Matt Pearson. Sandy, Matt, Ben Hamilton. He goes to Deacon Hill."

"When are you going to hold the raffle tonight?" Ben asked.

"Well, it's an ancient Woodbury tradition to hold all raffles after the third slow dance,"

Matt joked. "And the announcement of the winners has to be made in pig Latin," he added solemnly.

Cheryl and Mark arrived a moment later. Only a few people were dancing, so the group stood talking for a while.

Finally, Ben announced, "I'm going to get something to eat. Anyone want anything?"

"I'll go with you, Ben," Claire said.

But he shook his head. "You stay here," he said. "I'll bring you something." Then he disappeared into the crowd.

While the others began to dance, Claire stayed put, waiting for Ben. When he finally returned with cookies and punch, they talked for a while.

Then, slipping his arm around Claire, Ben said, "This is fun. I'm glad you asked me to come."

Claire smiled. "So am I!"

A moment later Warren Kruggel joined them. "Have you seen Rob?" he asked Claire. "I'm supposed to meet him at the punch bowl at nine o'clock to set up for the raffle. And I've got a problem—that drum I thought my dad could borrow from his lodge isn't available. We'll have to put the raffle ticket stubs in something else."

"Raffle ticket stubs!" Claire exclaimed, remembering that Ben hadn't given her the stubs from the fifty tickets he'd bought.

"They're in my car," Ben said. "I better run out and get them." With that, he took off.

"Isn't that the guy that knocked you over at the car wash?" Warren asked.

Claire nodded. "No comments, please. He's a perfectly nice guy. While I'm waiting for him to come back, want me to help you look for Rob?"

"Good idea," Warren agreed, and they headed off in different directions.

Claire wandered through the crowded gym, but saw no sign of Rob. Suddenly someone tapped her on the shoulder.

"Looking for me?" Rob asked, raising his eyebrows.

Claire frowned. "Where have you been?"

"How about a dance?" Rob asked instead of answering.

Claire felt herself blush. She looked around

for Ben, but didn't see him anywhere. "All right," she said. "*One* dance."

"Warren couldn't get the drum from his father's lodge," Claire said as they danced. "We'll have to use a big box or something instead."

"Good idea," Rob agreed.

At that moment Claire spotted Ben. As soon as their eyes met, he waved cheerfully. An instant later, the song ended.

"How about another dance?" Rob asked hopefully.

But Claire shook her head. "Sorry. Ben's back. Come on, Rob. He's got a mess of raffle ticket stubs to turn in. And we need to find a box somewhere." Without thinking, Claire took Rob by the hand and led him over to Ben.

"Did you get the stubs?" she asked Ben as soon as they'd reached him.

"Right here." Ben patted his bulging jacket pocket.

"I'll take them," Rob said. Suddenly, Claire realized she was still holding his hand and quickly dropped it.

"I'm going to check the art room for a big box," Rob added. "Catch you guys later."

"Shall we dance, then?" Ben asked as Rob left, his handsome face just inches from hers.

"Oh, yes," Claire said breathlessly.

The band had just started playing a slow dance. Ben opened his arms invitingly, and Claire stepped into them. Soon they were swaying with the other couples. When the song ended, Ben continued to hold her close. It was so wonderful that Claire wished the moment would never end.

Suddenly, Rob's voice came booming out of the huge speakers. "All right, everyone! Here's the moment you've all been waiting for. It's time for the big raffle!"

"Want to go?" Ben whispered in Claire's ear.

"*Now?* What about the raffle?" Claire asked. "Don't you want to find out if you or your friends won something?"

"You don't have to be here to win, right?" Ben asked. When Claire nodded, he said, "Well then?"

Claire looked quickly in Rob's direction. He'd found a big box, and it looked like Warren was going to do the actual drawing, so she wasn't needed.

"Okay," she said. "Let's go!"

Chapter Eight

On Saturday morning, Claire was sitting on a stool behind the cash register at Diaz Designs, trying to read a book for her history paper. Paul had spent the night at a friend's house and wouldn't be back until afternoon, and her parents were at an important business meeting in Minneapolis. Though she kept staring at the pages, Claire's mind was too full of Ben to concentrate on anything else. After they had left the dance last night, it seemed they'd talked about everything under the sun. By the time Ben took her home a little before midnight, Claire was almost certain that she was falling in love with him.

When she heard the shop door open, Claire expected to see a customer. But instead it was Sandy.

"So what's up?" Sandy asked eagerly, approaching the counter. "You and Ben disappeared before the drawing even started. Where did you go?"

"Nowhere in particular. We just went for a ride," Claire said, smiling at the memory.

Sandy said, "Ben won a dinner for two at the Wishing Well."

"That's nice," Claire said dreamily.

"Come on, Claire! Where did you two go?" Sandy demanded.

"We just went for a drive. We wanted to talk, and it was too noisy and crowded to talk at the dance."

Sandy whistled. "That sounds pretty serious!"

"Not really. We just talked about ordinary stuff, and he only kissed me once—at the door right before I went in."

At that moment the door opened again,

and Rob walked in. "I just stopped by to pick up the pendant and earrings," he told Claire. "Are they ready?"

"Not yet," Claire confessed. "My dad kind of got sidetracked this morning. He and Mom drove up to the city to meet with the managers of a couple of museum shops. They're talking about selling Dad's work there."

"Really?" Sandy asked. "That's great, Claire!"

"My parents are really excited. The pendant and earrings are almost done, Rob. Whoever won them can pick them up at the end of the week."

"Okay," Rob said. "Well, gotta go. I'm on my way to work. I just thought I'd check on the jewelry and make sure you were all right."

"Why wouldn't I be all right?" Claire asked, puzzled.

"You disappeared pretty suddenly last night. I was afraid you were sick or something. See you around." Rob started for the door, but before he reached it, Warren burst in.

"There you are!" he said to Rob. "I thought maybe I'd find you here."

Rob asked, "What's going on, Warren?"

"This!" Warren pulled a crumpled sheet of paper out of his jeans pocket and thrust it at Rob. "Deacon Hill is having a rummage sale tomorrow. It's going to be a big one, with lots of used, top-quality sports equipment. We're doomed!"

Claire stared at him. "What do you mean? What difference does it make to us?"

"Deacon Hill stole our idea, that's what," Warren replied bitterly. "They're going after that computer, too, and at this rate they'll probably win it! Just like us, they're willing to accept either Lind's receipts or money. And they're offering to give more credit for the receipts—fifty cents on the dollar."

"Why would they want that computer?" Claire asked. "I bet Deacon Hill has one for every student. Why are they doing this? It isn't fair!"

"They?" Warren repeated. "Don't you mean *he?*"

"What are you talking about?" Claire asked.

"Isn't the guy you were with last night named Bennet Harrison Hamilton III?"

"I suppose that *could* be his full name," Claire said.

"Well, he's the ringleader of this operation," Warren told her grimly. "That's what they told me when I called there half an hour ago."

"I just can't believe that Ben's behind this," Claire said sadly.

"It doesn't matter if Ben's involved or not," Sandy said, coming to her friend's defense. "It isn't Claire's fault that Deacon Hill decided to enter the contest. I mean, it's not like it was a secret or anything."

Claire tuned out, remembering all Ben's questions about the contest and the raffle. Suddenly it all made sense. Ben was going after that computer.

"Well, we'll just have to double our efforts," Rob was saying when she tuned back into the conversation. "They're getting a pretty late start. We've already completed two successful fund-raisers, and our own rummage sale is scheduled for next week."

"Maybe we should move it up," Sandy suggested.

"Good idea," Rob said. "Let's call an emergency meeting of the committee and see what we can come up with."

"I've got it!" Sandy cried. "Let's have a dinner meeting tonight, after you guys get off from work. Maybe Mark will let us make spaghetti at his house. Then we can meet in his basement. I'll call him right away." She dashed off, and Rob and Warren quickly followed.

After her friends had left and Claire was alone, she sat staring into space. Had Ben been using her to find out Woodbury High's strategy for winning the contest? Claire had been only too willing to tell him all Woodbury's plans. Of course, she'd never imagined that Deacon Hill would be interested in winning a single computer. Why hadn't Ben told her what he had in mind? Why hadn't he been honest with her? Didn't he care about her at all?

Claire's eyes filled with sudden tears. She would have to put Ben out of her mind, at least until the contest was over. She didn't want to be accused of fraternizing with the enemy, and the enemy was precisely what Ben seemed to be.

At the meeting that night, everyone agreed that the first step in their campaign to beat Deacon Hill was to check out the other school's rummage sale. Rob picked Claire up at nine-thirty the following morning, and they met Jonathan, Sandy, and Matt by the door to Deacon Hill's gym where the sale was to be held.

As they went inside and saw dozens of tables piled high with merchandise, Jonathan said, "It looks as if it's going to be a great sale. I wonder where they got all this stuff on such short notice?"

"Maybe they didn't," Claire said hopefully. "Maybe they've been planning this for a long time—even longer than we've been planning ours."

"Yeah, right," Rob scoffed, and Claire felt herself flush with anger.

The gym was beginning to fill up, and

among the crowd, she saw Deedee Chalmers, leading a band of Woodbury High cheerleaders. As Claire watched, Deedee wandered over to one of the tables and began talking to a dark-haired guy whose face Claire couldn't see. When he turned around, she gave a little gasp. It was Ben! She wanted to run over to him, but she knew her friends would never understand. They'd think she was a traitor.

After scouting out the sale for about an hour, the Woodbury High group decided it was time to leave. As Claire and Rob approached his car in the parking lot, they saw a boy in a Deacon Hill blazer walking by.

"This is some sale," Rob said to him.

The boy grinned. "Thanks to Ben Hamilton, we're going to win that computer Lind's is offering. You guys from Woodbury?" When Rob nodded, the boy said, "I guess you know about that contest, huh? Well, don't bother entering, because Deacon Hill's got it in the bag."

"Don't count on it," Claire muttered.

"What?" the boy said, frowning.

"She said, 'Good luck,' " Rob told him smoothly. "By the way, we were wondering where you got all the stuff you're selling."

The boy gave him a sly smile. "Some of the guys spent last week driving all over the place collecting junk at Goodwill stores and cleaning it all up. Great idea, huh?"

"Yeah, great," Rob said. "I suppose that was Ben Hamilton's idea, too?"

"His and Fletch's," the boy told him. "Those two are out to rule the school. They're only juniors, but you can bet that after this, they'll have no trouble winning the senior class elections. Well, nice talking to you."

Claire stared after him as he walked away, her head spinning from what she had just heard.

While Claire was doing her homework on Sunday night, the phone rang. For once, she got to it before anyone else in her family did.

"Hello—this is Claire," she said, and almost dropped the receiver when she heard a familiar voice.

"Hi, Claire. It's Ben. I saw you yesterday at

our sale, but every time I tried to catch up with you, you disappeared."

Claire swallowed hard. "Uh . . . that was a fabulous sale," she managed to say. "I heard you were responsible for putting it together."

Ben laughed. "Me and about twenty other guys. Are you mad at me because we're going after that computer of yours?" he asked.

"It *isn't* ours yet, and it's not yours, either," she pointed out. "As for being mad, it would be positively un-American to get mad about a little competition, wouldn't it?"

"Absolutely. May the best school win!" Ben said. "Listen, I didn't really call to talk about the contest. I wanted to know if you're busy Friday night."

Her heart pounding, Claire fibbed, "Just a minute—I'll have to check my calendar." She took a deep breath. It was only Sunday night, and already Ben was asking her out for Friday! That had to mean that he really *did* like her!

Then the reality of the situation came back into focus. Deacon Hill and Woodbury High were rivals in the contest. Claire was sure that Ben's intentions were honorable, but she didn't think the rest of the committee would see it that way. Then she frowned. She wasn't going to live her life the way her friends wanted her to. If she wanted to go out with Ben, she would, and the rest of them would just have to take it or leave it.

"It just happens that I'm free," she said into the receiver.

"Great!" Ben sounded elated. "I thought we'd see a movie. Pick you up about seven?"

"Sounds good," Claire said.

After she hung up, she flopped back into her chair. How would she ever be able to study now? How was she going to do anything at all except dream about Friday night, and wish it wasn't such a long way off?

Chapter Nine

The computer committee's next meeting was held on Monday during lunch in the cafeteria.

"Deacon Hill's sale was obviously a huge success," Rob said, "but the contest isn't over yet. We've got to come up with something really special for *our* sale on Saturday."

"I've got a couple of ideas," Val said. "There was sort of a carnival atmosphere at Deacon Hill yesterday, but they didn't take advantage of it. We could! For instance, Tremont Toys would probably donate a lot of balloons and we could sell them for fifty cents each."

"Great idea, Val," Sandy said.

"There's more," Val said. "Sinfully Sweet has an old-fashioned popcorn wagon that they rent out for parties. Maybe they'd let us have it for the day in exchange for mentioning them in our publicity. And we could add carnival games, clowns, the works! People will bring their kids, the kids will want to stay all day, and the parents will shop till they drop. We'll make a fortune!"

"I *love* it!" Rob said. "Claire, are you taking this all down?"

"Not yet," Claire admitted. She was rummaging in her purse for paper and pen when Warren came running up to the table. He was obviously upset about something. "I've got bad news," he said grimly. "We can forget about our rummage sale."

Everybody stared at him. "What are you talking about?" Sandy cried.

"The contest is over," Warren said. "Deacon Hill turned in their receipts this morning. They've won!"

"How do you know?" Claire asked, stunned.

"I heard it on the radio in the art room. I

went up there to see if I could make more posters for Saturday. The radio was on, and WWTT was making the announcement."

"Maybe it's a mistake," Rob offered hopefully, but Warren shook his head.

"No way. I called Lind's right away," Warren told him. "It's for real, all right."

"What are we going to do with all the rummage we've collected?" Cheryl moaned. "My dad said it has to be out of our garage this weekend."

"We've got to go ahead with the sale," Mark said. "Okay, so we didn't win the computer. But we can still help the Food Bank."

"But what about accepting Lind's receipts instead of cash?" Sandy asked. "That won't work anymore."

"True," Mark said. "But we could accept food donations, like canned goods and stuff like that."

"Okay, then!" Rob said. "Full speed ahead with Operation Food Bank!"

Ideas came fast and furious from everyone at the table except Claire, who kept busy writing down what was being said. She felt terribly guilty about agreeing to go out with Ben even though she knew it wasn't her fault that Deacon Hill had won the contest. But she was sure she was in love with Ben, and nothing was going to make her change her plans.

"Claire, wait up! Have we got terrific news!"

Claire turned around to see Rob and Warren hurrying down the hall toward her. She glanced up at the wall clock. It was nearly three. Her bus would be leaving any minute now.

"What is it?" she asked. "I have to catch the bus." Claire's parents were going to Minneapolis as soon as she got to the shop. The museum contracts were ready to be signed, and she didn't want to make her parents late for their appointment.

"Forget the bus," Rob said. "I'll give you a lift. We can talk on the way. Come on, Claire. This is big—really *big*!"

"Oh, all right," she said. "So tell me already. What's the big deal?"

"Deacon Hill cheated!" Rob and Warren shouted as they swept her out of the building.

Claire stopped in her tracks. "Says who?"

"Don't you think it's pretty obvious?" Rob asked.

Claire frowned. "Not to me."

"I warned you, Rob," Warren muttered. "Claire probably *helped* them, for Pete's sake!"

Claire gasped, and Rob turned on Warren. "Would you just shut up?"

Warren threw up his hands. "Sure." He started walking away, saying over his shoulder, "I just hope you figure out who your *real* friends are before it's too late, Meyers!"

Claire was fuming as she and Rob walked in silence to his car. She had done nothing to give Deacon Hill an unfair advantage! What was wrong with Warren, anyway?

Once they were buckled into their seats and Rob began to drive out of the parking lot, he glanced at her and said quietly, "You don't believe it, do you?"

Claire shook her head violently. "No, I

don't! They might have gone all out to win. Maybe they even had the wrong reasons for wanting to win. But that doesn't mean they're cheaters. I think we should be good sports about the whole thing and face up to the fact that we lost fair and square."

Rob sighed. "You don't know the whole story. Remember that guy we ran into in the parking lot after the rummage sale on Saturday? Well, he's the one who told Warren they cheated. His name is Earle Wyman Young, Junior. He calls himself E.J. He's a good guy, and he's felt bad about this whole thing."

"But why would he tell Warren? I'm sorry, Rob, but none of this makes any sense. If we pursue it, we'll only look like soreheads. I say drop it. Getting a computer isn't worth it."

Rob pulled to a stop in front of Diaz Designs, and Claire got out. "I've got to go," she said. "It's a big day for my parents. I've got to take over so they can leave."

"Sure," Rob said. But he sounded as though he didn't believe her.

As Claire hurried into the store, she heard the Chevy roar off down the street.

"I'll get it!" Paul cried when the phone rang shortly after he and Claire finished their dinner that evening.

They both assumed that the call was from their parents, telling them about the finalization of their deal.

"Hello?" Claire heard Paul say eagerly. Then a second later, he added, "Oh, sure. Just a second." He held out the receiver to her. "It's for you. Some boy."

Claire sighed as she took the phone. She had a feeling it was Rob, calling to tell her she was wrong, and she really didn't want to talk to him.

"Hello?" she said.

"This is Ben, Claire. How are you?"

"Ben!" Claire sighed with relief. "I'm fine. How about you?"

"Good," Ben said. "Actually, great. I guess you probably heard about us winning the contest."

"Yes, I did. Congratulations."

"Thanks. I didn't think it was over yet, but after we'd counted up all our receipts, we realized we'd won. I just wish both schools could have won. That's really my only regret. But then, I guess the world doesn't work that way."

"No," Claire agreed. "I guess not."

"About Friday," Ben went on. "About our plans, I mean. Do you think I could have a rain check? We're going to be doing some celebrating here tomorrow night. I guess I could skip it, but . . ."

"Oh, no," she said quickly. "Go ahead. I understand. We can go to a movie anytime. You don't want to miss your victory celebration—I know I wouldn't miss mine if Woodbury had won!"

"Are you sure you don't mind?"

"I'm disappointed," Claire admitted, "but I'll get over it."

"You're wonderful, Claire! Look, I'll call you soon, okay?"

"Sure. Talk to you soon."

"Bad news?" Paul asked as Claire hung up.

"Not really *bad,*" Claire told him. "Disappointing, but not bad."

Suddenly the phone rang again, and Claire picked up the receiver eagerly. Maybe it was Ben calling back to say he'd changed his mind! *A date with you,* he'd say, *is far more important than celebrating with a bunch of guys.*

"Hi, honey. It's Mom," Mrs. Diaz said. She sounded giddy. "We did it, Claire! Dad signed the papers. Diaz Designs is on its way. Tell Paul we're picking up a cherry pie and vanilla ice cream to celebrate. Don't either of you kids dare go to bed before we get home, okay?"

"That's great, Mom," Claire said. "But you better talk to Paul yourself. He's standing right here and he looks like he's about to explode." Claire handed the phone to her brother, then left the kitchen. She needed to be alone for a bit. She didn't want to be feeling sorry for herself when her parents got home.

Chapter Ten

"Are you and Matt going out tonight?" Claire asked Sandy on Friday afternoon after school as they boarded the bus to go home.

Sandy shook her head. "It's Matt's grandmother's birthday today. His family is having her to their house for dinner."

Claire said, "Good. Then you can go to the movies with me."

"Okay," Sandy agreed. "What do you want to see?"

Claire said, "I don't care." She was pretty sure her mind wouldn't be on the movie, anyway. She was going to be thinking about Ben.

"You look depressed, Claire," Sandy observed. "What's wrong?"

Claire shrugged. She didn't want to talk about Ben. Claire hadn't told Sandy about the date Ben had made, so it seemed a little foolish to tell her now that he'd canceled it.

"I suppose you know that Warren keeps telling everyone who'll listen that Deacon Hill cheated," Sandy said as the bus turned up Claire's street.

"I wish he'd stop," Claire said. "The least we can do is be good losers."

"I don't know what to think," Sandy mused. "It *does* seem that they won awfully quickly."

"Can we please change the subject?" Claire begged.

"Okay. Let's talk about how we're going to get to the movie. Your dad or mine?"

"Mine," Claire said. "He's so excited about his contracts, we'll be able to talk him into anything."

* * *

"Just for me?" Claire squealed that evening at supper. "You're buying a computer just for *me*?"

"Actually, for the business. But you can use it whenever we aren't using it," her mother promised, smiling.

"What about me?" Paul chimed in.

"You can use the new computer, too, Paul," Mr. Diaz promised.

"Whenever *I'm* not using it," Claire said.

"Well, let's get these dishes washed so we can get you to the theater in time, Claire," her father said.

"Oh, no," Mrs. Diaz said. "You two go on now. Paul and I will do the dishes."

"Great!" Claire cried. "I'm out of here."

She dashed into the bathroom and quickly brushed her teeth, combed her hair, and put on some pale lipstick. Then she slipped on her parka and joined her father in the living room.

"All set?" he asked. Claire nodded. "Then we're off to pick up Sandy."

When they pulled to a stop in front of Sandy's house a couple of minutes later, Claire ran up to get her friend. Sandy came to the door all ready to go. Like Claire, she was wearing jeans and a bright-colored jacket.

"Hey," Sandy said, immediately noticing the look on Claire's face. "When you got off the bus this afternoon, you looked downright gloomy. Now you look like you swallowed the sun. What gives?"

"We're getting a computer," Claire said excitedly.

"We?"

"My family. My parents. Me!" Claire exclaimed happily.

"That's great, Claire," Sandy said, smiling. "Now you won't have to fight with Rob over the one at school. Who knows? Maybe the two of you will finally get together."

Claire made a face. "Don't count on it. He's not too happy with me right now."

The girls chatted on the way to the theater. When Mr. Diaz dropped them off, they stared up at the quadruple marquee.

"Which one do you want to see?" Claire asked.

Sandy frowned. "I don't know . . ."

"Claire! Sandy!"

They turned around to see Rob and Warren walking toward them. Apparently they weren't mad at each other anymore. Claire wondered if they were still mad at *her*.

"Hi, guys," Sandy said. "What movie are you going to see?"

Warren grinned. "The one about the guy with the blades for fingers. It's fantastic."

"Tell them how many times you've seen it," Rob said.

"Actually, this will be my sixth," Warren confessed.

Sandy whistled. "If it's that good, I guess we'll see it, too. Okay, Claire?"

But Claire didn't answer. She was staring at the box office where a dark-haired boy was buying tickets. It was Ben Hamilton, and standing very close to him, her arm laced through his, was Deedee Chalmers.

"Claire?" Rob said. He put his hand gently on her shoulder. "Are you all right?"

"We had a date," Claire murmured.

"You and Ben?" Sandy stared at her. "You mean for tonight?"

Claire nodded numbly. "He broke it." She'd let herself be used, she'd let herself be lied to, and she'd let Bennet Harrison Hamilton III make a fool of her!

"Maybe now you can see the truth about him," Sandy said.

"Let's get our tickets and go in," Rob suggested.

"Wait," Claire said. "Sandy's right. I *do* see the truth. You were right, Warren."

Warren looked surprised. "What was I right about?"

"You were right about Deacon Hill. If they really did cheat on that contest, I think we should blow the whistle on them."

Rob shook his head. "I don't know, Claire. I've thought about what you said before and decided that *you* were right. Making a big stink after the fact would be poor sportsmanship."

Claire looked deep into Rob's eyes. "I was wrong," she admitted. "It isn't poor sportsmanship, Rob . . . it's honesty. I didn't believe that Ben was capable of cheating before because I didn't want to believe it. But he's cheating right now . . ."

"So he was capable of cheating before," Sandy finished for her. "What are we waiting for? You've got your car, don't you, Rob?"

"All right!" Warren cheered. "Let's go to Deacon Hill and expose those guys! Maybe we can win that contest after all!"

Claire slipped her hand into Rob's. He gave her a surprised look but didn't pull away. Instead, he tightened his grip, and Claire felt a current travel through Rob's hand to her own. Her cheeks grew warm with excitement.

Fifteen minutes later, Rob pulled into Deacon Hill's parking lot. He parked his red Chevy at the back of the lot and everyone piled out.

"Where do we start?" Sandy asked. She looked nervously around the well-lit campus.

"First, we find E.J. I just hope he's still willing to help us," Rob said. He turned to Warren. "How do we find him, Warren? I hope you know."

"We'll try his dorm room first," Warren said. "That's where I talked to him before. Luckily he doesn't have a roommate."

"Who's E.J.?" Sandy asked.

"Earle Wyman Young, Jr.," Claire told her.

Sandy shrugged. "Never heard of him. But that doesn't mean anything. Lead on, Warren!"

Warren led them toward a cluster of ivy-covered buildings that were obviously dormitories.

"We've got to be careful," Rob warned. "We don't want to get E.J. in trouble."

"Not to mention ourselves," Sandy added.

"Don't worry," Warren said. "You three wait out here. I'll find E.J."

He entered the nearest dorm while Rob, Claire, and Sandy drew back into the shadows to wait for him. A few minutes later, Warren was back with E.J. two steps behind.

"It's all there," E.J. whispered. "It's all in the print shop. Ben and Fletch and the others printed up enough receipts to make up the difference between what they had and what they needed. I can show you how they did it. I can even show you how to tell the real receipts from the bogus ones. The paper's a little different, but if you weren't looking you wouldn't notice, which is just what those guys were counting on."

"That's counterfeiting!" Sandy exclaimed.

"Shhh!" E.J. hissed. "If the other guys find out I turned them in, I'm dead meat around here. Come on." E.J. started walking, motioning for the others to follow. He finally stopped in front of a building. "The print shop's in here."

They entered the building through an unlocked side entrance and slowly made their way down the dark corridor. Finally, E.J. stopped, opened a door, and flicked on the lights.

"Look at all these computers!" Rob said, his voice filled with awe.

"Just look at them all. Why would Ben and the others bother cheating just to get another one?" Sandy asked.

"They didn't do it for the computer," E.J. told her. "Ben wants to get elected president of next year's senior class. Winning this contest was part of his campaign strategy."

"So where's all the evidence we're supposed to find here?" Warren demanded impatiently.

E.J. walked to a metal trash can and began riffling through its contents. "Bingo!" he cried suddenly. He was holding a bright pink strip of paper, which he waved at the others.

"What's that?" Sandy asked.

"Evidence," Warren said, taking the slip from E.J. "This paper is just like the special cash register tape Lind's purchased to use during the contest."

"It's almost the same color," E.J. added. "But not quite. Obviously the people at Lind's didn't notice. But when you bring this in and they get out the receipts Deacon Hill turned in, they'll see that it's true. Only some of the receipts are legitimate . . ."

". . . and the rest are counterfeits!" Sandy finished for him.

E.J. nodded. "I told them they didn't need to cheat. If we'd just put in a little more time, we could have won fair and square."

"I guess we'll never know," Claire commented. "Deacon Hill will undoubtedly be disqualified from the competition after this."

E.J. sighed. "You know, it's really a shame. This mess will probably drive the townies and the Hillies even farther apart than they were before."

"Oh, I don't know about that," Sandy said. She gave E.J. a smile. "You've shown that not all Hillies are bad guys."

"That's right," Rob agreed. "You've got a lot of integrity, E.J."

E.J. blushed, obviously pleased. "Thanks," he said. Then, turning to the others, he added, "Come on. Let's get out of here!"

"Where are we going now?" Claire asked when she, Rob, Sandy, and Warren got back to Rob's car. She looked at her watch. It was eight o'clock. Her father wasn't going to be back at the theater to pick them up until nine.

"Lind's," Rob said. "We're going to move on this right now."

A few minutes later, Rob pulled into the Lind's parking lot. He parked and everyone got out and hurried inside.

"We need to speak to the manager," Rob told the first person he saw wearing the Lind's uniform.

The young woman pointed to an office marked "Manager." "The night manager is in there," she said. The clerk walked over to the office and knocked. A second later, an older woman opened the door.

"These kids would like to talk to you, Ms. Ortes," the clerk told her.

"Thanks, Shelly. Come on in. So, what can I do for you?" Ms. Ortes asked as they hiked into her office.

"We brought you this," Rob said. He handed her the phony receipt.

Ms. Ortes looked at it a moment. "I don't understand. What *is* this?"

"A fake," Warren said. Ms. Ortes looked confused.

"What he's trying to say," Claire told her, "is that Deacon Hill cheated in the computer contest. A lot of the receipts they turned in were created in their own print shop."

Ms. Ortes looked skeptical. "That's a pretty serious accusation. Why are you so sure?

Where did you get this, anyway?" She waved the crumpled receipt at them.

Rob proceeded to explain the whole story.

"Well," Ms. Ortes said with a sigh as soon as he had finished, "we're obviously going to have to look into this. I'll leave a note for Mr. Stevens, our daytime manager." She asked for their names and phone numbers and wrote them down. "Of course, I'll have to keep this," she said, pointing to the counterfeit receipt.

"When do you think Mr. Stevens will call us?" Rob asked.

"I can't say. Tomorrow is Saturday, our busiest day. It might not be until Monday," Ms. Ortes warned.

"Can we ask you not to mention this to anyone until then?" Rob asked.

"I don't plan to talk about this with anyone but Mr. Stevens," she assured him.

"Where to now?" Rob asked as they walked back to the car a few minutes later.

"I guess you better take all of us home," Claire said. "My dad was going to pick us up at the theater after the show. If we get home quickly, we'll be able to catch him before he leaves."

"Then I'd better take you home first," Rob decided.

When they got to Claire's, Rob pulled up to the curb in front of the store, and she started to get out.

"Wait," Rob said. "I'll walk you up."

"You don't have to," Claire said.

"I know," Rob said. "I want to. I'll be right back," he told Sandy as he got out of the car.

"Take your time," Sandy said cheerfully.

Rob joined Claire on the sidewalk. When they reached the alley, he took her hand. Claire couldn't help laughing.

"What's so funny?" Rob asked. He sounded hurt. Claire gave his hand a reassuring squeeze.

"I'm laughing because this is Sandy's dream come true," Claire told him. "She thinks we belong together."

"What do *you* think, Claire?" Rob asked. He stopped walking and turned so that they faced each other. Claire's heart began to beat faster.

"Do you think you'd consider going out with me?" Rob asked softly.

"Are you actually asking me for a date?" Claire asked in mock astonishment.

Rob let go of her hand. "This isn't going to be easy, is it?" he asked.

"Do you want it to be?" Claire countered.

"I'll tell you what I want," Rob said. He took both of her hands in his.

Feeling suddenly bold, Claire whispered, "Don't tell me, Rob. *Show* me."

He pulled her toward him and she shut her eyes just as Rob's soft lips brushed hers.

"Oh, no!" a familiar voice yelled from above. Claire pulled away from Rob. It was her father! Claire looked up just in time to see a streak of orange come bolting downstairs and into the alley. Claire giggled. Taxi had escaped!

"Grab him, Rob!" Claire said. "Quick! Before he gets out of the alley."

Rob dove and pinned Taxi to the ground.

"Got him!" he said, and handed the struggling cat to Claire. "I better go," he said. "I've got to take Sandy and Warren home. But I'll definitely see you tomorrow."

"Right," Claire said. She let him pull her close and closed her eyes, anticipating another kiss. But before their lips could actually meet, Taxi let out a howl.

"What's going on down there?" Mr. Diaz hollered. Claire and Rob exchanged a frustrated look, then they both started laughing.

"Nothing, Dad," Claire called. "I'm on my way up."

"Next time I try to kiss you," Rob whispered, "*no cat!*"

Claire smiled. "It's a deal."